James W. Steele

To Mexico by Palace Car

Intended as a guide to her principal cities and capital, and generally as a

tourist's introduction to her life and people

James W. Steele

To Mexico by Palace Car
Intended as a guide to her principal cities and capital, and generally as a tourist's introduction to her life and people

ISBN/EAN: 9783337194475

Printed in Europe, USA, Canada, Australia, Japan

Cover: Foto ©Andreas Hilbeck / pixelio.de

More available books at **www.hansebooks.com**

To Mexico by Palace Car

A CORNER OF THE MARKET PLACE.

TO MEXICO

BY

PALACE CAR.

INTENDED AS

A GUIDE

TO HER PRINCIPAL CITIES AND CAPITAL, AND GEN-
ERALLY AS A TOURIST'S INTRODUCTION
TO HER LIFE AND PEOPLE.

BY JAMES W. STEELE,

AUTHOR OF "CUBAN SKETCHES," "FRONTIER ARMY SKETCHES,"
ETC., ETC., ETC.

———————

CHICAGO:
JANSEN, McCLURG, & COMPANY.
1884.

CONTENTS.

PREFACE 7

CHAPTER I.
PRELIMINARY 11

CHAPTER II.
MEXICAN SCENES AND CHARACTERISTICS . . . 17

CHAPTER III.
GOING THERE 32

CHAPTER IV.
THROUGH MEXICO 47

CHAPTER V.
THE CITY OF MEXICO 72

CHAPTER VI.
THE VALLEY OF MEXICO 84

PREFACE.

MEXICO, save to the very few, has until very recently been an almost unknown country. Among the latest and most surprising achievements of American energy must be counted the construction and final opening of the Mexican Central Railway, forming a continuous line through the heart of the country from Paso del Norte to the Capital. The republic is now open for the entrance of whomsoever will, and her chiefest cities are connected by a continuous line with the entire railway system of the United States.

It is unquestionably the greatest event, save one, in the stormy and sombre history of our sister State, and to Americans themselves is of only secondary importance.

Fenced by impassable barriers for some three-hundred years, this old, rich, quaint and isolated empire has suddenly become the coming country of the capitalist and the tourist; a land in which, by the invitation of its people, we have already begun an endless series of beneficent and bloodless conquests.

The Mexican Central would be almost valueless alone. Other gigantic enterprises on our own soil preceded it and made it possible. Energy, money, and foresight are the prophets of a practical age, and the long lines of steel that were laid across plain and mountain, through uninhabited silences, and amid danger, hardship, and Indian hostility; which had their beginnings in the populous towns of the Missouri Valley, and an unknown ending in the far Southwest, have now demonstrated some striking reasons for their being. Among these, undoubtedly, is that which is continuous with the Mexican Central from its northern end, the Atchison, Topeka and Santa Fé, itself among the longest lines of railway in one direction ever built, or that will ever be built, on the American continent.

The northern side of Mexico is her nearest side in all senses. Her most valuable neighbor is our own country. Differing from her in everything but form of government, internally strong, enterprising, advanced in ideas and education, wealthy and adventurous, we are yet akin to her in national sympathy, allied to her by strong commercial interest, and intensely interested in her advancement. We are, in sober truth, the only neighbor from whom she has aught to hope. To us, Mexico is the coming country, if there be any. She is accessible, as she has never been before, hopeful, expectant, cordial with a sincerity the wisest had scarcely hoped for in this century, and seemingly fearless of the magnified and unreal dangers of political alliance, and abandoning all the ancient antagonisms of race and custom, asking for no passports and making no enquiries, she invites every comer from the land of her ideals and hopes, to the palms and pyramids, the gray towers and tropical gardens, of a capital that may be as old as Thebes, is as quaint as Tangiers, as foreign as old Spain, and as new as the newest American territory to all modern things.

It is, finally, but fair to recall the well known fact that a brief characterization of a people is a difficult task. What is here set down is but the condensation of hundreds of impressions, but they are stated *de buena Fé*, and after having eaten salt with nearly all classes of a heterogeneous population, who were, however, while the brief association lasted, all Mexicans and Americans, all courteous, and, I am in duty bound to add, among the most agreeable of good fellows.

TO MEXICO.

CHAPTER I.

PRELIMINARY.

THE American is reputed the great mod-ern adventurer. There is no civilized country to which he has not gone or to which he does not intend to go. Every year he pours himself out upon Europe like the swarms of Attila, with his women-folk and personal belongings.

But, as yet, he has not extensively visited Mexico, though probably the most interesting of all regions, and to be seen with the least inconvenience.

The country has heretofore presented many obstacles to even the adventurous American mind. With his usual astuteness, he has dis-

missed the subject with the quick conclusion
that it would not "pay." It was the land of
countless revolutions and political uncertainties. It was colored with memories of San
Jacinto, The Alamo, Buena Vista, and the
exploits of General Santa Anna. All Mexicans, judging from the few specimens seen by
us, were innocently but very erroneously
deemed to belong to the variety called "greas-
ers." We all recall certain sentences from the
speeches of Thomas Benton, and certain half-
forgotten narratives of the surviving veterans
of that unnecessary series of brilliant skir-
mishes called by us the Mexican war. And,
until very lately, the country could boast of
but one railway,— from Vera Cruz to the Capital,— and that single evidence of internal
enterprise necessitated a sea voyage to the
fever-haunted port which has no harbor, and
has long been distinguished for clumsy light-
erage, "northers," and watery accidents. The
country has been fenced in by rocky barriers,
mountain chains, and immense distances more

impassable than any sea; by lack of information concerning it, and by all the differences
of race, language and custom.

This has been so far changed that the
requisites now of a most delightful journey
are merely a through ticket and return, and
a sleeping-car berth. The time required is
about the same as that stated from any given
eastern point to San Francisco, possibly a few
hours less.

In people, climate, scenery, and a strange-
ness that is astonishing as pertaining to the
North American domain, the country undoubtedly repays a visit. It is not going to a
"resort," and in no reasonable sense can a
journey thither be called a visit. It is not a
locality, but a country. Winter and summer
the climate remains nearly the same, a region
of tropical latitude, but immense elevations.
There are senses in which Florida, the West
Indies, the Bermudas, offer no comparisons.
Saying nothing of the Capital, there are cities
in Mexico whose very names are unknown to

Americans, hitherto fenced in by the barriers
of nature, only now accessible even to the
majority of Mexicans by rail, containing from
forty thousand to ninety thousand inhabitants,
where palm trees grow in the plaza, tropical
fruits are the usual products of every month
in the year, and yet where blankets are comfortable every night. All the delicacies of the
garden, and every product of the field, grow
almost side by side with cotton, cane, limes,
bananas, and a hundred differing fruits, whose
very names are unknown to the majority of
mankind. Yet there are no tropical diseases,
and none other than those common to hu-
manity everywhere, while a light overcoat is
desirable every evening.

Mexico is preëminently the land of mountains. Near and frowning, or blue and ethe-
real with the haze of distance, they are everywhere before the eye, until the senses become
accustomed to grandeur, and tired of inac-
cessible majesty. Ragged sierras, towers,
castles, cones, seamed and scarred veterans of

the age of fire, fence the horizon in.   Among them lie valleys where the vertical sun shines scarce half the day, where villages nestle and mysterious waters flow, and where the only aspiring thing is the tower of the inevitable church, shapely and beautiful even in the most squalid village.

Notwithstanding, the changes are almost infinite.   You may go from the Capital, which to all Americans, as to all Mexicans, is the centre of a system, by rail to Cuautilla or Yantepec, or to Amecameca, at the foot of his serene and smoky majesty, Popocatapetl.   If you are adventurous you may even climb that elevation of some nineteen thousand feet, and for once in all your life, standing amid eternal snows, you may look down into the fervid heart of our common mother.

But everywhere you will encounter a quaint, primitive, slow and picturesque people.   The Mexican at home stands as the sixth race; unlike all others in appearance, gait, language, and probably blood itself.   Street

and village scenes afford the stranger a pan-
oramic amusement which does not fail him
in weeks of association. Customs, industries,
habits, mechanical operations, with industrial
contrivances unknown to all the world beside,
are everywhere. You may surprise your inner
man with strange beverages, and accustom
your palate to dishes hitherto not included
among your necessaries of life. You may
witness the decaying exploits of the bull-ring,
the excitement of the cock-pit, or hear the
strains of Italian opera. But everywhere and
always, you are wrapped in a climatic brill-
iance that never fades, save when it gives
place to the flashes of stars that seem nearer
and brighter than ours. It is the perpetual
glow of a land where winter never comes, and
whose people, time immemorial, worshipped
the sun.

CHAPTER II.

MEXICAN SCENES AND CHARACTERISTICS.

FOUR-FIFTHS of the people of Mexico are Indians; that is to say, pure Aztecs, totally unlike the "noble Red Man" of our latitudes. The remainder are of mixed descent, and, in a few cases, Castilians. The common and natural idea is, that being a Spanish conquest, Mexico, like Cuba, should have few or no Aborigines left, and that Mexicans are the descendants of the conquerors and of Spanish blood.

But the Indian blood is not the cause of any social or other distinction, save that it is considered, if anything, somewhat better than the Spanish. Benito Juarez, the most lamented of their presidents, was an unmixed Aztec. Porfirio Diaz, the strongest Mexican of his times, and in many respects the Gen-

2   17

eral Grant of his country, is of mixed blood. Everywhere the Aztec face, unmistakable in its pathetic features, goes with the best and worst types of Mexican character. Spain, her glory, her tyranny and her dominion, have seemingly left but the faintest marks upon Mexican personal characteristics. Religion, somewhat modified, language, and the Moorish architecture, are her bequests to Mexico, and are apparently all that is left to mark the brilliant conquest of Cortez.

Of the whole number, a larger proportion of the population than of any country except Italy, seem to be very poor. This has grown to be largely personal habit, but is also due to the stress of circumstances in a country so isolated that she has lived over and over again within herself, producing what she could consume, and no more. There are other causes, destined to be discussed in all their fulness very soon, one of which undoubtedly is a system of laws which permits the holding of vast bodies of land by one

COUNTRY BRIDE.

19

individual or family, exempt from taxation. There has been for some sixty years, and until within a limited time, an almost continuous internecine dissatisfaction, sometimes accentuated by an uprising first in one distant community and then in another. Affairs in this respect have greatly changed. Troops may now be very quickly sent to districts which they would not formerly reach in a year, if at all. Nobody seems to have any great apprehensions. There is now great interest in outside affairs, and a general desire to imitate all that is good in our own republic. The railways have immensely stimulated the desire to make, to sell, to ship, to travel, to see with the natural eye the country that has shown sufficient confidence in forsaken Mexico to expend her millions there. The conversation of the intelligent Mexican on these subjects is sometimes almost pathetic. Inaction and laziness, at least, are not, as has been so often imagined, the cause of financial stress on the part of the masses. Every

Mexican toiler is so from early youth. Boys are stone cutters and burden bearers from twelve years. The peasant's gait is quick and all his movements active. He is a notoriously fast walker. Slight in figure and thick set, he will, and often does, carry a burden of three hundred pounds, and go off with it at a jog trot that I had always imagined the Chinaman held an exclusive patent upon. There are no drays. To be a "cargador" seems to be an ambition of Mexican peasant youth. Three men, and sometimes two, will carry a piano a dozen squares.

In truth the ordinary Mexican seems undaunted by tasks that would be undertaken by no other man. A crate of crockery, of vegetables, of fruit, of anything, may be discerned jogging rapidly up some steep road, so huge that the bearer is quite invisible, and he has tirelessly borne it across mountain and valley in a country where leagues are notoriously long. Long trains of donkeys wind through the country, laden with sugar, cotton, wool, hides, wood, stone, and a single native plods behind the train. He has come perhaps a hundred miles, and eaten for a day what would not furnish the average American a single meal. Loafing, except of the absolute variety, and systematically in the sun, is quite unknown. Frugality is not a virtue, but a thing of lifelong practice and necessity.

Every Mexican, of every grade and class, is a courteous man. Ask him a question, and he invariably gives you the best answer at his command. He is generally willing to spend time and effort for your accommodation. He is never embarrassed. The girl by the roadside never blushes and never runs away. Look at a Mexican gentleman, and he is wont to smile and salute you. Ask him a question on the street, and he will shake hands with you at parting. People whom you never saw before, and will in all probability never see again, will willingly show you through museums and libraries, give you their time for an hour, shake hands and bid you good-by, merely because you are a stranger, and during the whole time never ask you a personal question. The stories with which every new-comer is regaled and enlightened upon his arrival, are seldom borne out by the experience of three weeks. The author has been among some of the hardest crowds in the byways of the Capital, where the yeasty odor of *pulque* mingled itself with indescribable smells to which the two-and-seventy of famed Cologne were as roses, and was never molested, threatened, touched, or even looked at sidewise. Nevertheless, every traveller will be duly informed of the hatred of all natives for the "*gringo*," and warned that they will steal the ring from his finger and the cigars from his pocket. There are thieves, and some very ingenious and inveterate ones. I would myself, and perhaps so would the reader, like to be informed where there are not. You may come as near tempting fate in Mexico as in any country.

Americans are in certain things the most inconsiderately impatient of all people. Mexico is the slowest country on the globe, with the exception of Spain, Italy, Portugal, Russia, and all South America. There are about sixty millions of people on this side of the Atlantic who speak the Spanish In all America the English tongue is in the minority. If you go there you will have all the better time if you do not try to reform the country. Avoid the impatient gesture, the disgusted look, and the pushing demeanor which accomplishes nothing. It is the land of *mañana* and *luego*. You must wait more or less; since you must, it is as well to do it patiently.

On the other hand, order, neatness, system, regularity, are not studies in Mexico. There are no chambermaids, no American brooms, no private boarding houses. Male servants clean your room and make your bed. You pay so much per diem for a room and one candle, and are expected to furnish your own soap, which is an article of luxury not the cheapest. You may eat where you choose, regularly, irregularly, or not at all. Living in the Capital is not cheap, nor indeed very dear, averaging something like four dollars per day, for all necessaries. By rule, breakfast comes at 12 M., and dinner at about six. There is a cup of coffee in the morning. There are many good hotels of their kind, the Iturbide being a magnificent building, and the San Carlos, in the same square, good enough. There are also a large number of bad ones, which state of things is not confined to Mexico entirely. A stranger can tell as much by the price as by anything; a good room can hardly be got for less than two dollars per day. In towns like Querétaro, Aguas Calientes, or Zacatecas, hotel bills, including everything, are about three dollars per day.

Beds, always for a single person, are good and clean, but if one cares for a soft pillow, it is well enough to carry a small one in all journeys through the country. In outlying towns the idea of what constitutes a hotel is, to say the least, unique. In most places the chances are the tourist must camp, or wish he had done so. The ancient *meson* exists in many places. It is a building into whose open court the diligence drives through a castellated gateway. Mules, pigs and domestic fowls occupy the place together. A water-tank is in the centre. Around the sides are the rooms. Each has one door, no windows, no beds, no furniture of any description. The antique wayfarer furnishes everything and carries it with him, and rents the room for a single night. It reminds one of the scenes in Don Quixote.

There are now too many lines of railway to interesting places, for the visitor to be under the necessity of often using either diligence or *meson*. If it becomes absolutely necessary to go to some out-of-the-way place where the pilgrim may become a social discoverer, it is best to hire the universal burro-train and Mexican, "camp out," be your own purveyor of distances and fare, and, aided by the novelty and the kindly climate, have a time to be remembered.

Nearly all of Mexico that the tourist will wish to visit has an elevation of from five to seven thousand feet, and though far within the tropics, may be said to be never oppressively hot, and never really cold. There is never a need of great variety in clothing. One may almost wear the same garments for as long as they are whole, for all seasons. It is best to bring with you the same clothing, including underwear, you would use in the autumn months in the Northern and Middle States. It will be found that it is better too heavy than too light, better of solid material than of texture particularly fine, better of light colors than of black or very dark. There are nevertheless days in midsummer when it is quite too warm for comfort. The rule may be fairly stated thus ; always warm in the sun, always cool in the shade, always chilly at night-fall. There is no day in the Mexican year when light flannel underwear ought not to be worn.

In the matter of gayety, the city of Mexico

presents a striking contrast to that other tropical capital, Havana. She has flowers innumerable all the year; a climate of indescribable brilliancy, and yet is a sad city. Mexican shops close at seven o'clock in the evening. The conventional bride's dress is the gayest I have ever seen in Mexico. The striking colors of the sunlit street arise altogether from the sunshine and the universal *serape*. It is quite as well to leave off the usual American custom, and come to Mexico with but little baggage. If it is desired above all to enjoy oneself and see the contrasts of Mexican life, a slight equipage makes it all the easier. An ordinary business suit is all that is required. Ladies, of course, are expected to have more luggage, but the railways all charge a rate for baggage that is not carried in the hand, and the street-dress of northern cities, or a travelling suit, is all that is really required.

It may be at first a matter of surprise that the average Mexican seems to know so little of his own country, and to have so little local pride in its history and interesting antiquities. It is not strange to him; he has always been there, and has never thought much about it. It is not yet a show country. When this feature changes, it will, as usual, change too much.

Another strange thing is, that with an advancement in art that surprises every visitor, the country has no literature. The galleries of the Capital are filled with specimens of the old and new schools, many of which would be masterpieces in any country. Yet, so far as I have been able to discover, there is not a publishing house in the republic, and the three or four book-stores of the city are filled with French works, either scientific or novels.

The railways are a new thing, except the Vera Cruz line, which was some twenty years in building, and, finished, is less than three hundred miles in length. As yet the average citizen has no adequate appreciation of their fateful results to him and his country. While

intensely interested, and very hopeful, he is
yet a man who has no thrills, and dreams no
dreams, who in times past has frequently
broken out and done something politically
desperate, but who usually accepts the inevi-.
table with that peculiar fatalism fortunately
quite unknown to the Saxon. Many of his
ways are such as will not strike the visitor as
those that are to be imitated with profit, and
many of them are admirable instances of the
adaptation of man to fate. But he is a man
who is by nature picturesque, even in rags,
and a Mexican crowd is a brilliant assemblage
in the white sunshine of the Mexican street,
without regard to the quality of the decora-
tions. The tourist comes upon the native
now, in all his villages and by-ways, in the
condition in which he has been for two hundred years. Such an instance of primitiveness is not to be met with elsewhere. He is
awakening from his *siesta;* but the quaintness
of his race and kind will probably never
entirely leave him. The deep peace which

broods upon all his hills can never entirely depart, and the yellow glory will never be dimmed. He is the still vigorous descendant of a powerful race whose idols he has abandoned and whose language and history he has forgotten, but whose ancient dominion he still holds; the Mexican, almost the pathetic last man.

CHAPTER III.

GOING THERE.

THERE are at least two classes of travellers into whose hands this little volume may chance to fall: first, those whose time is not especially limited, and who desire to see Mexico for the gratification of the highest form of curiosity of which men are capable, and for the novelty and change to be found in its climate and people. Second, those who go there for business purposes, whose release from other business is temporary, and who desire to pass by all secondary points, "taking in" only the most prominent. Yet there is one thing unavoidable by anybody, and that is the journey thither. It therefore seems necessary, in any effort to convey information about Mexico, to begin at the beginning. In this connection the author begs leave to state facts as he believes them to exist, and as they have occurred in his own experience, regardless of the claims of other routes than the one taken by him, any and all of which may have their points of just distinction. The all-rail route is, as a matter of course, the preferable, and the more nearly all-rail a journey is, in the immense distances now traversed by thousands of travellers, the better. The Pullman car has been made in late years to attain to immense and hitherto impossible distances, without delay, accident or repair. Systems of baggage-checking that are complete beyond anything known in other countries, make the change from one car to another a matter of little inconvenience when it does rarely occur. Vera Cruz, as a port without harbor or landing, and the railway line running thence to the City of Mexico, have been in existence many years without greatly affecting the travel to or from the country, and without, in any sense, changing that isolation which has made Mexico for hundreds of years the remotest corner of Christendom.

3

The line which, in an almost direct course
to the southwest, has for its chiefest object
the Mexican Capital, is the Atchison, Topeka
and Santa Fé. Though not directly, its course
is general toward El Paso for the whole of
the immense distance between that point and
Kansas City, which is its eastern terminus.
To the latter place it will be necessary to
come some day, in any event. The town is
not a beauty. It was, some twenty years ago,
nothing more than "Westport Landing," on
the unpicturesque banks of the Missouri.
From that miserable hamlet it has grown to
be the most important city of the West—not
so much in size, though rapidly attaining that,
but as the depot of a great industry, the re-
ceiver and distributor of countless thousands
of cattle and swine, the absorbing nucleus of
a trade that in a few years will be able to supply the world with beef.

Soon after leaving Kansas City, and becom-
ing fairly settled in one's section for a journey
that is more like a voyage than a tour by rail,

A COMPETITOR OF THE LOCOMOTIVE.

35

the enormous distance covered by the Atchison, Topeka and Santa Fé becomes a matter of reflection. It has a strange story. It was definitely projected and persistently built through a howling wilderness that, as a result few men of that day would have been bold enough to prophesy, it has made to blossom as the rose. For years it continued its westward course, forgotten almost by the stockmarket and the newspapers. It extends from Kansas City to the port of Guaymas on the western coast of Mexico, and to El Paso del Norte upon the northern and nearest side to us of that republic, where its track is continuous with that of the Mexican Central, which is, in effect, the extension of its line unbroken to the City of Mexico. Its length, including its Colorado line, and other branches built by it, is about two thousand four hundred miles. Its line directly and continuously travelled in a journey from the eastern terminus at Kansas City to Mexico, extends across the farms and orchards of

eastern Kansas, traverses the Arkansas Valley*
for nearly four hundred miles, crosses the
southeastern corner of Colorado, traverses the
entire length of New Mexico from north to
south, and finally places its passengers across
the southern boundary of the United States
and upon foreign soil, and behind a locomotive whose headlight glares still southward
across the limitless meadows of Chihuahua.

It is natural that the ancient, the tradi-
tional, the moss-grown, should attract the
interest, and affect the sensibilities of the
average American. We have not many of
those things to display, and seek them in Ger-
many, Italy and the mother country. But we
have, in compensation, those most wonderful
pictures of human progress, that are impossi-

---

*Some fourteen years ago the Arkansas Valley in Kansas was
traversed by the writer, principally accompanied by an intelligent
mule. Through its whole length there was not a soul or sound.
There was not while this line was building. It was the grass-
grown "American Desert,"—useless, irredeemable. There are
now living there more than half as many people as the famed, rich
and beautiful Valley of Mexico contains after a civilized occupation
of some three centuries.

ble to any but Americans, and to any century but this. Hundreds of us who have been everywhere else have never seen it; thousands more have no just conception of it. Students of history, to whom the epocha of the world are as familiar as the alphabet, take no note of the times in which ten years make a century, and the days of a single generation change all the features of a life that has no traditions and no past. A single crossing of the vast theatre of these affairs, a single view of the widening edges of this human flood, is almost enough to change one's conception of his relations to his age, and modify his firmest views of the capacities of his race.

In this sense, not regarding views of mountain scenery, and the wide expanse of plains that are like solid seas, and looking only upon that spectacle denied to men until this age,— the magnificent processes of the erection of an empire,—a journey through the West for the first time is a wonderful thing, and the

tourist to Mexico may congratulate himself
upon its being included in his passage.

The journey upon which the traveller has
entered is, as stated, as much a voyage as a
journey, lacking only uncertainties, sea-sick-
ness, and general unsteadiness. The city of
Mexico is south of latitude twenty, Kansas
City is north of thirty-nine. It is a journey
of near two thousand miles if it lay in a line
as directly north and south as the course of
the wild goose. There is not a break in the
line of about two thousand three hundred
miles. A section of a Pullman car becomes a
residence, and the companions of the journey
are as those who have lived upon the same
street with you for years.

It is cold: the storms of the northern winter have locked the world within those icy
bars that are the similitude of death. In two
days you may be beneath a glowing sun,
whose rays, at an altitude of five to seven
thousand feet, illuminate a world of blue
mountains, silent valleys, and distances whose

immensity is lost in purple haze. It is warm,
glittering, and gives you the impression of
changelessness, and that it never rains. You
are far above the highest mountains of home.
The top of Mount Washington is something
you would not note, and might look down
upon. There are mountains around, and still
above you, and their tops are scarcely distin-
guishable from the clouds that sail in the alti-
tudes of another world.

In those two days you have had unrolled
before you some of the most extraordinary
aspects of American civilization. You have
passed through those gigantic progresses that
are more wonderful than the tale of Aladdin's
lamp. You have seen in new lands and un-
tried fields a wealth, intelligence, and content
that in the first half of the century, and the
last quarter of the eighteenth, would have
been a marvel if accomplished in fifty years.
The white walls of school houses; the roofs,
and monstrous architecture of elevators; cities, little and ambitious, or big and indepen-

dent; streets crowded with the wagons of the country folk; smoke from tall chimneys; hedges, orchards, herds, homes, are upon every hand. There is the sound of bells and the screaming of whistles, and human crowds that are all Americans, with the same language, laws, ambitions and hopes that other Americans have, yet are no more like eastern people than eastern people are like French.

You have crossed the Great American Desert; at least if you have not there is none. It is so much a desert that it is the great grazing country of the United States, teeming with enormous and growing wealth. It comprises all northwestern Texas, western Kansas, southern Colorado, and eastern and southern New Mexico. It is dotted here and there with immense herds, owned by companies whose capital stock runs most frequently into the half millions, and who must in a short time control the cattle market of the world. The line of the Atchison, Topeka and Santa Fé seems to cross this immense space from

northeast to southwest. You may see occasionally beside the track a little ranche, the
queer structure known as a "chute," a cowboy
in his paraphernalia, and on all sides cattle,
the plain, the hills, the sky and loneliness.

Then comes New Mexico. It is easily said,
but it is by no means new. These rambling
villages were named before the American rev-
olution, and the capital is the eldest town of
North America. You have exchanged your
leagues of plains for the smell of pines, and
the sharpness of mountain air. Queer villages nestle in the valleys, and bronzed and
weather-beaten faces and an unknown tongue,
nondescript garments, and an ancient routine
of life, indicate the oldest civilization under
the American flag. It is an incongruous mix-
ture. The Yankee town has grown up beside
the track, while the rambling adobe one lies
sleepily behind it. The burro train divides
the highway with the red-and-green American
wagon. The Mexican woman, hiding her features in the time-honored *rebosa*, creeps tim-

idly beside the jaunty northern girl along the
street, presenting the most opposite of femi-
nine contrasts. The old life is not changed
and the new life is not hindered. Adobe takes
upon itself glittering door-knobs, glass windows, and shingle roofs, while the civilized
mansion has for its nearest neighbor the primeval dwelling, whose earthen roof has shel-
tered successive generations.

There is too, the unchanged dwelling of the
Pueblo, that hive of communistic industry
that seems indifferent to all that comes, perpetually changeless. Between the ashen
stream beside whose banks he has lived a
thousand years, and the long lines of railway
track, his village stands, a changeless memento of a time so old that its years are uncount-
ed. Through all that time may bring, the
ancient man seems composed and serene, the
victim, through hundreds of years, of the
Apache, the Spaniard, and finally of American
civilization.

But it is not a voyage in which there is no

touch of *tierra firma*, unless the voyager so de-
sires. Near at hand are at least two places
where one may rest for a day, a week or a
month. One of them is Las Vegas Hot
Springs,* a charming watering place and
health resort, the grounds and hotels of which
are owned by this company, and the other of
which is the ancient city of Sante Fé.

The stopping place for Las Vegas Hot
Springs is the little city of Las Vegas, from
which there is a train of the same line, con-
necting closely, and going to and returning
from the hotel several times per day. The
distance is only some six miles, by the valley
of the little river Gallinas.

Just below Las Vegas, and immediately beyond the famous Glorieta range, is a station
called Lamy, after the bishop of Santa Fé.

---

* The fine hotel at Las Vegas Hot Springs was burned in Janu-
ary, 1884. The same company is now engaged in the erection of a
new one, with, if that be possible, some improvements upon the
old. Before this accident, in which the loss, except as insured, fell
entirely upon the company, these Springs had attained a wide reputation, both for beauty of situation, and health-restoring proper-
ties.

From here there is a ride of seventeen miles, often said to be one of the finest in America, up the mountain and among piñons and cedars, to Santa Fé.

This old and most interesting city is a fore-taste of Old Mexico. For near three centuries it has been the political and religious capital of the picturesque territory which the old country did not lose until yesterday,—say about 1850. For a few days it is interesting, full of adobe palaces and crumbling churches, of legends and reminiscences. Tesuque (Ta-soo-kee), a village of the Pueblos, lies a few miles away, and is well worthy of a visit.

Long before this the voyager will have left the eastward flow of waters, crossed the mountain barrier through the tunnel and steep incline of Raton pass, and entered the valley of the Rio Grande—the *Rio Bravo del Norte* of the Spaniards. To one who visits the region for the first time, the scenes are quaint, almost comical. Burro trains, adobe castles, higgledy-piggledy villages, are every-

where. Sunshine of the yellowest variety
seems to shine always. It is a world of black
lava blocks, gaunt cacti, frowning ranges of
sierras, and profound and unbroken peace.
There are sometimes running streams that
seem to have been mysteriously coaxed up
hill, and gardens whose green luxuriance surprises the eye.

After these scenes, occupying more than
two days of uninterrupted travel, and so
quickly passed by a train whose incongruous
noise seems to awake echoes that were forever
sacred to Aztec gods, the sun sets upon *Jorna-
do del Muerto*, for the last time, in this journey,
under the American flag. In the morning you
are in El Paso, and before you lies the wide
domain of Mexico.

CHAPTER IV.

THROUGH MEXICO.

THE ancient and sleepy town of El Paso del Norte is the utmost northern point of the Republic. It lies, an agglomeration of adobe houses embowered in vines and trees, on the southern bank of the Rio Bravo del Norte,— known to us as the Rio Grande. In ancient times the stream may have better deserved its designation, and have really been the "Mad River of the North." Owing to the drainage of its rolling flood for the uses of irrigation, a view of it from the railway bridge shows the modern traveller only glimpses of yellow water lying between bars of brown sand. Mexico happens to own only about seventy miles of navigable stream, and only one shore of that. A little grandiloquence in the matter of naming what she has must, therefore, be excused.

But the Rio Grande is not the only thing at El Paso; the other striking feature is contrast. The old town on the southern side lies dreaming. The modern one on our side has a "boom." Another thing is climate. Situated neither far north nor extremely south, with an elevation of some five thousand feet above sea level, the invalid or semi-invalid who is tired will find here that almost perpetual brilliancy for which these latitudes are famous, with an average winter temperature of about 65°, and an air which, in summer, is always cool at night and in the shade. Fruits abound, especially the Mission grape, apricots, plums and pears. Mountains lie on every hand, and the scenery, while not striking, is pleasant and not tiresome. It is a brisk place, and there is always the ancient and sleepy town across the river to visit by way of change; always the queer admixture of the old civilization with the new.

Lastly, there is the comfort of a first-class hotel. The "Grand Central" is modern, new,

LA SEÑORA DEL HACIENDA.

and very complete. Expecting very little in that line, the tourist will find here the best hotel, excepting that at Las Vegas Hot Springs, west of Kansas City.

As to the old town across the river, reached by street cars, the visitor who stops over will be impelled to go there. It is nothing to what comes after in Mexico, but is at least a first striking specimen of Mexican primitiveness. It has always been a neglected frontier, a crossing-place for the ox teams of the ancient traffic, and a great place for the prosecution of the legitimate Mexican industry of smuggling. Its cathedral is the only adobe one I know of in all Mexico; was undoubtedly skipped in the age of church building, and is only interesting from its association with the faith of primitive worshippers for about two hundred years.

Here, of course, the tourist must "pass" the custom house,— fit beginning for the enticing pilgrimage which lies still to the southward; unnecessary adjunct to the jealous portals of every nation. But no passports are necessary; nobody asks you for any documentary evidence that you are not a bandit, and there seem to be no annoying restrictions as to personal baggage.

Except where, by a series of remarkable engineering gymnastics, it climbs the mountains at Zacatecas, and the notched rim of the Valley of Mexico, the Mexican Central road seems, strangely enough in so mountainous a country, to traverse a vast plateau. The sensation in this respect, from Paso del Norte to Chihuahua, about two hundred and twenty-five miles, is peculiar. Cones, peaks, castles, ridges, lie on every hand. The train heads straight for some huge bulk, and always quietly slips by, uninterrupted for the most part, by cut, fill, or steep grade. Almost the whole distance, studded with such knobs and projections as have been mentioned, and sometimes diversified by glassy-looking lakes, is covered by a heavy growth of gramma grass, and is a pastoral country on an enormous scale. Many thousands of cattle are passed, grazing near the track; the telegraph poles are rubbed until they are sometimes smooth and oily, and trails run in all directions. The country really does change its character at the Rio Grande. The peculiar plateau formation is not characteristic of the northern side. Yet, in this first stage of a journey in which the traveller is to be so forcibly reminded that he has left the United States, there is no noticeable difference in personal surroundings. Every moment the star-spangled banner is growing more dim and distant in the North. You are under the red, green and white of a country that it is an unfortunate part of your education to believe antiquated, uncertain and capricious. But cars, passengers, conductor, rails, locomotive, are all American. They have "come across," to use the current expression, and do not seem particularly to regret it. Perhaps, however, if you go into a forward car, you may find some of your fellow Americans, with brown faces and excessive hats, and wrapped in crimson-barred serapes until their faces are scarcely visible.

Nor will there as yet be any necessity of resorting to *tortillas* and *chile con carne*. At noon there is a dining station very much like those you have always been accustomed to, and a very good dinner is served in the American style.

Chihuahua may be regarded as the first Mexican city. It contains some 18,000 inhabitants, and is a permanent departure from the adobe style of architecture, which has always been regarded by us as the inevitable and unavoidable building material of the Mexican. When you come back, and intelligent people ask you if the city of Mexico is built of adobe, you will privately smile, and wonder how it was that you yourself once had the same notion.

Chihuahua, for various reasons, deserves a brief visit. It is, in the matter of public spirit and enterprise, a good deal Americanized, and all the ideas of the place are advanced to a notable degree. There is a handsome plaza, an aqueduct of some two-hundred-and-twenty years' standing, many mines of paying rich- ness, a cathedral whose elaborately carved front has been much admired, and a vast vari- ety of Mexican scenes and ways, very sugges- tive of what is yet to come.

The place was once captured by the Ameri- cans, and held as long as suited their conven- ience. If it be daylight, the traveller may see just north of the city, and close to the track, a shelf of ground above the plain where the three brown mounds still stand which were the Mexican earthworks at the battle of Sac- ramento. This, in the light of later days, was not much of a skirmish, but it is very well that it was no more than that.

The place was also captured by the French, which is the same thing as saying that it was made to come under the rule of Maximilian. There is a bell in the tower of the cathedral which, during some one of these military vicis- situdes, was pierced by a ball. It still rings, and is not considered as having its usefulness greatly impaired. The tourist, after hearing all the bells, and before finally emerging from Mexico, may question within himself whether it has not been really improved by the accident.

After Chihuahua the line of the road lies for some two hundred and fifty miles through a region that is, in a sense, a desert. Rugged mountains fence in stretches of cactus-grown plain. Long vistas of level lands stretch away among the peaks and ridges almost as far as the vision extends. Occasionally, appearing in a most unexpected manner, are districts of cultivated fields, green in midwinter with growing grain, and having in view at any season all the antiquated and curious processes of Mexican agriculture. Pastoral country on an enormous scale is not wanting, and the seeming desert is grazed by innumerable goats. You wonder what they do with so many, the goat being very far from your idea of the representative of abounding wealth, in his best estate. Well, they are killed by the thousand for their hides. The hides are dressed in a manner that makes them look like fine brown cloth, and used in the making of the Mexican breeches.

Occasionally rivers are crossed, of which the Nazas is a fair example. Where such is the case, it does not take much of a district to hold and support ten thousand people. As has been stated, the country has few rivers, and all are drained almost dry by huge *acequias.* Surrounded by chains and ridges, the valleys of Mexico lie like green gems in a setting of bronze. Their products exceed per acre anything known of fruitfulness in the North, and the population they support is enormous.

It begins to be perceived first in these regions, that corn, cotton, wheat, cane, barley, grow almost side by side. In most cases continuous crops of a kind follow each other in rapid succession through all the year. A crop of barley is harvested and another is sown.

Cotton will never compete with that grown by us, because the plant is a perennial, and becomes a tree, shortening its staple every year. It is cut down and the field replanted once in six or eight years.

A hundred miles south of Chihuahua, is Santa Rosalia, famous among Mexicans for its sanitary hot springs. It is reported by the few foreigners who have yet visited it to be, as to the quality of its waters, probably the finest health resort in America.

In these regions the population is almost entirely gathered in communities. There is a ridge, or sierra, or some vast agglomeration of sterility, and then, with the suddenness of turning a curve, appears a densely populated valley, which seems to have dropped from some other world.

In this region, and in the course of a few hours, are passed the Florida Valley, the ranch region of Jimenez, the laguna country, Lerdo, and Jimulco. It is in a Mexican sense, a fine country; to the traveller a constantly recurring puzzle as to whether it is rich, poor, or merely indifferent. It is to be remembered that the process of irrigation solves all agricultural uncertainties. Ranches, far and near, sometimes attaining to the dignity of respectable towns, sometimes only a cluster of hovels, are seen in mountain glimpses. Sometimes the country, as far as one can see, is an appalling desolation, untenanted by even the ravens. Yet even here the faint lights which indicate human habitation are seen twinkling through the night, and in daytime groups of Mexicans rise like ghosts among the mezquite and cactus. Trains of donkeys, bearing curious loads, plod patiently along white roads. Here and there around the horizon are seen the tall and slender columns of white dust, undulating and contorted, but never broken by the mysterious wind, that mark as an especial feature every Mexican landscape.

In these solitary fastnesses vegetation takes upon itself the most unusual and fantastic forms. There is nothing that is not thorny.

The little pear cactus, so often seen in gardens and pots with us, becomes here a tree that is the desert Caliban of vegetation, with a trunk and branches as large as those of an oak, and with huge green lobes, two feet or more in diameter, for leaves. It is as thorny as ever, and more so, but bears a blood-red fruit which, once plucked and peeled by the horny and accustomed hands of the Mexican, is called "tuna," and is good.

The bunch of slender green lances which everyone remembers who has ever been to New Mexico, called by us "Spanish bayonet," and which is the "soap weed," or its near relative, is here a tree sometimes forty feet high, on whose huge and scaly branches the "lances" stand in grotesque tufts for leaves. It becomes, indeed, a member of the extensive family of palms,— a kind of poor relation.

Mezquite, known all over the Far West as a plant whose gnarled and crooked roots are used as fuel, is here, upon tens of thousands of acres, a not unhandsome tree, the groves of which remind one of an abandoned orchard of immense extent. There is, where these grow, a thick sod of grass, green or brown according to the season, no undergrowth, and a gently undulating landscape. It will never, in all probability, be the fate of the reader to encamp in these solitudes. If he should, he would be surprised to hear the songs of innumerable mocking birds in the early morning, in the leafy covert of the mezquite desert. Jackass rabbits, out of gun shot, quizzically regard you, and the tufted heads of the mountain quail glide from cover to cover like small spectres. Sometimes, but rarely, the antlers of a black-tailed buck appear above a clump, or his tawny hide goes like a flash past an opening.

In any village in these regions one is astonished to find piles of yellow oranges, bananas, limes, and fruits one does not even know the names of. In no case may it be predicted what a range of rugged hills may hide, or what green valley lies unseen in the heart of apparent desolation.

Tanks, excavated by hand to catch the rains and hold water during the dry season, are common. One of the resources of the country is shown in immense herds of "burras," with colts, sometimes numbering many hundreds.

Often, where the silence of the wilderness seems to close around impenetrably, the shapely tower of the universal church may be seen above the hills, and a visit thither would disclose a town, its rule of life the traditions of two centuries, and all its hopes bounded by the church door and the gate of the little *campo santo* which ends all. Through such scenes, destined to be entirely unnoticed and unknown by the railway traveller, now pass the rattling trains waking the primitive silences with a shriek,— a flash of the present century across primeval dreams and shadows.

It is rather a queer sensation to look from the railroad station down into Zacatecas. It

is about half way from El Paso del Norte to
the City of Mexico, a mining town of about
80,000 inhabitants, compact, closely built, the
houses seemingly an immense number of red,
green, blue, and yellow bricks set on edge.
For it is necessary always to look down into
it, and to see it requires not only elevation
necessarily, but distance. It is wedged so
closely into its narrow valley that it has
foamed over the edges, and crept up the hill-
sides in little terraced clusters of adobe. It
swarms with people of the true and ancient
Mexican type, sombreros, serapes, sandals,
buttons and all. All around it lie piles of
slag, openings into hills, square inclosures,
tall chimneys, indicating the ancient and
present industry of the place, which is silver-
mining. On Sundays, should the visitor hap-
pen there on that day, he will find the streets
almost impassable because of the crowds,
and every corner of the place turned into a
market. Every man is busy chaffering with
his neighbor, and all the world is in good

humor. The list of articles bought, sold, peddled, supposed to be wanted, considered too high, bought at two prices, swapped for something else, would make up a list not found classified in any custom house of the known world. There are no wheeled vehicles to be seen. What is not carried on the native's back is relegated to his brother carrier, the donkey. Altogether it constitutes a scene not to be found elsewhere in any land.

The contortions of the railway line in reaching Zacatecas add something to the interest of the visit. "Mule shoes," as bends of that form are called in the West, are not only common, but in one or two instances double. The oddity of the Mexican scenes below, which are but hinted at here, combined with a railway mountain climb which has few equals, makes Zacatecas a point of interest, even if the tourist should spend but a day in its curious environs.

The best hotel is called the "Zacatecano," and the visitor is inevitably the occupant of the cell of some departed nun, as the fine building was once a convent, the beautiful chapel of which is now used by the native Presbyterians as a house of worship.

All Mexico is street-car crazy, but the most remarkable branch of the "tram-via" system undoubtedly will be found in operation here. Its grade up to the railroad station is something near eight per cent., and on the opposite side of the town about six per cent. Through these narrow and crowded street; six good-sized mules to the car are made to go at a keen gallop. There are two drivers, a brakeman, and two conductors, besides, I think, a man whose extra-official functions are somehow connected with the management of a long whip. Once at the top of the hill, the mules are taken off and the car is turned loose laden with passengers, running down the steep incline at something like twenty miles an hour.

From the crest of the hill, on the opposite side of the town from the railroad, is the finest view possible of the wide and characteristic Mexican landscape, a view which, once impressed upon the mind, is not likely ever to be forgotten.

AGUAS CALIENTES comes some four hours below Zacatecas, and is reputed justly one of the attractive places of Mexico. There are in all likelihood about forty thousand people here. The streets are wide, the plazas handsome, the architecture good, and the climate not so cool as places near by of higher elevation.

The principal attraction is the *aguas calientes*, from which it takes its name. The oldest and best of the baths are reached by street cars through the Alameda, a shaded walk. The springs have a temperature of 106°, and rise strongly through the black sand in the bottom of the old-fashioned square stone baths. The arrangements are primitive, but clean and comfortable.

There is a newer and more pretentious bathing establishment in the town called, by

5

way of distinction from the first, the *Baños Chicos*. The buildings are quite pretentious, but the bathing arrangements are bad, and the water in its course through the pipes becomes too cold.

The cathedral, on the plaza, contains the most sonorous bell in the republic. Considering the almost studied dissonance of the bells of Mexico, the visitor will remember with no small degree of satisfaction *La Campana de San Pedro*.

The old and somewhat dilapidated church of *Nuestro Señor de Los Encinos*, on the outskirts, contains fourteen pictures, life-size, painted by Lopez, about one hundred years ago. They are well worth a visit, though neither priest nor people seem to be aware of the fact.

From Aguas Calientes downward, or upward actually, the valleys are wider and more numerous, and the arid tracts grow more infrequent. Rushing streams of water, coming from some unknown head, frequently surprise the eye. Many districts are of evidently enormous richness, and in midwinter are as green as June in the northern States.

Some sixty miles below Aguas Calientes is the little town of Encarnacion. Here is the only iron truss bridge on the line of the Mexican Central road. It spans a chasm of great depth, through which runs the Encarnacion River,—the most diminutive streamlet ever called by the name of river.

SILAO is a place where the tourist begins to see something of the agricultural beauties of Mexico. The town sits placidly in the midst of a smiling valley, green always, and cultivated like a northern garden. The neatness and resulting success of Mexican agricultnre are here exemplified.

The amiable custom of the citizens of Silao is to come every day to the depot when the train passes, as they would go riding or visiting. There are many pretty women among them, if the fact is considered important by the average American visitor, and it is sincerely hoped that no arrangement of the time tables will cause the trains to pass in the night.

QUERÉTARO comes next as a place of interest, the last one directly upon the line north of the Capital. Leon and Guanajuato intervene, though not immediately accessible, or without some delay. Leon is probably the next largest city of the republic after the Capital, and is wholly given up to manufactures, principally of leather. It is an exceedingly interesting place to visit, though it boasts of no picturesque features. Guanajuato is distant some leagues from the main line, and is reached by branch from Silao, lacking some four miles. It is entirely a mining town, often stated to be the most important one in the country. It divides that distinction with Zacatecas.

Referring again to Querétaro, it will be found by the visitor to be in a peculiar sense worthy of an inspection. Bathed perpetually in an atmosphere almost tropical in midwinter, plentifully supplied with all the products of perpetual summer, neither the railroad nor anything new seems to have the effect of modifying the character for which it has always been famous. It is in Querétaro always about A.D., 1640, and four o'clock in the afternoon. The narrow streets may or may not lie at right angles with each other. They are narrow, dense, and with so few windows that they come near seeming to be long streets of blank walls. It is the reputed conservative town of Mexico, and the tower of defence of the church party. The place has a lasting memento of this peculiar reputation in the little barren hill in the suburbs, where Maximilian, Miramon and Mejea were shot together. It is as lonely a spot as lies anywhere under the sun, this *Cerro de las Campañas*, and that particular spot on its brown slope which is marked by three little wooden crosses, saw the end of a brilliant scheme to strangle an established government and plant a European empire on transatlantic soil. I chanced to walk thither beside a donkey on which rode an old woman and a huge basket. She was garrulous of the event, and gave the details of the doings of that time with a vividness the histories do not attain to.

From Querétaro there is a general upward tendency of the track until you attain the edge of the rim that bounds the famed Valley of Mexico. The scenery is by turns grim in its brown ruggedness, and smiling with perpetual roses. The valleys are full of orange, lemon and plantains. The line makes some surprising turns, and there is another "mule-shoe," or more than one. The one dining station that is yet to be passed is delightful of its kind, at San Juan del Rio, and the only one on any American line where the dinner is served in courses, with thirty minutes to eat it in, and with an abundance of tropical fruits for dessert.

Passing the crest which is the rim of the valley, the line is cut in the wall of the ancient canal which was digged to drain the waters of the lake, in, or on the edge of which the city which is now Mexico stood. It is useless and dry now, but remains a curious relic of the time when there was a Venice in the heart of Mexico, and when the streets of the Capital were traversed in canoes.

A PERPETUAL GRIND.

CHAPTER V.

THE CITY OF MEXICO.

ON the authority of so distinguished a traveller as Bayard Taylor, the City of Mexico, with its surrounding valley, may be pronounced to be one of the loveliest scenes of the civilized world. The same places do not always produce the same impressions upon every individual, but it is safely to be concluded that there is at least no similar scene. No adequate description of it has ever been written, and the reader is advised not to expect one here. Extensive reading on the subject fails to give any impression like that obtained by the first glance at the reality. The only even partial embodiment of it I know of, is condensed into two paintings in the gallery of the School of Arts, at the Capital, and they do not include any view of the city itself.

MEXICAN PLOUGHMAN.

The City of Mexico, with a population variously estimated at from 225,000 to 300,000, is situated upon ground that was once the bed of a lake. The lake was what is now the Valley of Mexico. It was never intended by nature to be other than a body of fresh water, and nature is constantly rebelling against the inadequate plans of making it what it is; the site of one of the most beautiful capitals of the modern world. The lowest part is still Lake Texcoco and her sisters. Some of the finest buildings bend downward in their centres, owing to want of solidity in their foundations, and there is not the means of efficient sewerage. Lake Texcoco at low water is only some six feet lower than the city streets. Chapultepec, Tacubaya, Peñon del Marques, Guadaloupe, are but rocky islands whose tops once protruded from the shallow waters.

The city is small in area, stands on perfectly level ground, and from any of the eminences named above, presents the remarkable view which has elicited the encomiums of every traveller. The same effect is produced by a view from the roof of the College of Mines, or that of the National Library, and is supplemented by the seemingly near and snow capped peak of Popocatapetl, and the glassy waters of the lake.

The streets are some sixty feet wide, with wide sidewalks, and the city lies closely built in regular squares. The buildings are mostly of two, though sometimes of three or four stories. The square in front of the Cathedral, called the Zócalo, is the place of universal resort, though there are two or three others, handsome and clean, but not so well kept nor so expensively ornamented.

It is the city of churches, as Mexico is un-questionably the land of churches. Their towers, always handsome, assist very much in making up the general view. It was also once the city of nunneries and monasteries, all of which are now suppressed, and the buildings used for schools and other purposes, all sec-ular.

The following memoranda of places of interest in the city itself are offered more as hints or suggestions to entire strangers, than as a complete list of all places worth a visit. One might spend an entire week in the streets, and feel at no loss for entertainment. When time does not press, it is decidedly better to be in no great haste. It must be understood that even where scenes are not always picturesque, or even agreeable, they are quite strange, and new to all American conceptions of life. There is an endless procession of them, and coupled with the charms of sunshine, quiet, and rest, the visitor will find that from three days to three months may be profitably spent without any great anxiety about dates, history, or exact information. Of interesting public buildings, there are:

THE CATHEDRAL.—A description of which is hardly necessary, as it is almost in the centre of the city, and open always. Against the western wall, and close to the ground, is built the celebrated Aztec Calendar Stone, figured in every book of travel. To say truth, it is not precisely known whether it was a calendar stone or intended for some other purpose. The greater wonder is that it was ever preserved, as all the emblems and paraphernalia of heathendom and all the written and pictured records of the natives were destroyed in holy zeal during the first years of the Conquerors. It may be of service to add that this Cathedral is conceded to be the largest ecclesiastical edifice in America.

EL PALACIO DEL PODER EJECUTIVO DA LA NACION.—Which would be in English the national White House, or the Executive Mansion; is the largest building in the city, occupying one entire side of the Plaza Mayor, or Zócalo. It is ancient, but not particularly prepossessing. It was not by any means constructed for its present uses, for it belonged to the family of Cortez until 1562, and was then purchased by the king of Spain for the use of his viceroys. Nevertheless it has, in one way or other, been the government building

through all the vicissitudes of some three
hundred and fifty years.

COLEGIO MINEREA. (College of Mines).—Is
the most elaborate and expensive edifice
ever constructed by the Mexican government,
and one of the most sumptuous of educational
buildings. Begun in 1784, it was not finished
until 1813. It is quite completely equipped,
has extensive and interesting mineral cabinets,
and is well worthy a visit.

EL MUSEO NACIONAL. (The National
Museum).—Was established in 1822, and is de-
voted to Natural History, Archæology, and the
Ancient History of Mexico. The collections,
antiquities, and cabinets of natural history,
are large and curious. Aztec remains, and
large photographs of the ruins of palaces or
other public buildings existing to this day at
Uxmal, Mitla and Chitzen Itza, would seem to
indicate that the Aztec tribes at the time of
the conquest were almost or quite as advanced
in civilization as the Conquerors themselves,
and yet practised to an extent desperate and

exterminating, all the rites of human sacrifice.

For in the court yard lies the huge stone that could have been intended for no other purpose. It is a block of volcanic rock shaped like an enormous mill-stone, and about nine feet in diameter by some four feet thick. It is as elaborately carved as though done by the best modern tools. There is in the centre of the upper surface a basin to catch the blood, and a deep gutter to carry it off. Much use must have been given it, as one side is worn perceptibly smoother than the other.

But among all the gods, tools, instruments, and other grotesque things that lie in the court-yard, the best piece of carving is only a domestic utensil, apparently meant to be used for the unromantic purpose of boiling meat. It is a kettle holding some twenty gallons, shaped precisely like our modern cast-iron ones, with ears for pot-hooks on each side, and a lug for convenience in tilting it on one of the opposite sides. The whole is cut in stone

as hard as iron, and the thickness of the
vessel is not more than twice or thrice as
great as that of cast metal. It required years
of work to make that one kettle. It is a curious illustration of the cheapness of toil and
time among the Aztecs.

EL CONSERVATORIO DE MUSICA. (The Con-
servatory of Music).— It occupies the building of an ex-Jesuit university, which was
begun as long ago as 1551. It is an institu-
tion for governmental instruction in music
of a high order, and a very great credit to
the country.

LA ACADEMIA DE SAN CARLOS. (The Acad-
emy of San Carlos).— This is dedicated to
instruction in the fine arts, and is also an
extensive and interesting gallery of paintings. There is nothing in Mexico that will
better repay several visits. What is called
the ancient school of Mexico (of art), fills the
visitor with surprise; surprise that a country
so crude, isolated and generally *atrasado* in
all the advances of modern times, should

have produced such pictures, and more than a hundred and fifty years ago. There is also the *escuela moderna*, very fine, but with the exception of a few that are exceedingly good, seeming to the visitor to have somewhat the modern French tone.

It ought not to be omitted, while briefly upon the subject of art museums, to state that these galleries also contain an original each of Murillo, Leonardo da Vinci, Ingres, Carreno, Ribera, and Teniers the elder; also supposed and probable Vandycks and Rembrandts.

LA BIBLIOTECA NACIONAL. (The National Library).— This is established in what was the church of San Augustin, a fine building, and perfectly suited to the uses of a great library.

The feature which especially strikes the visitor is the great number of parchment-bound volumes, some of them in manuscript. The dates of a few, casually taken up, were 1639, 1570, 1708, 1562. Many, if not all these

6

books were once private property, and some of them are curiously branded with a hot iron upon their ends, and with a variety of devices, the same in system, though not in extent, as the branding of cattle in Texas.

EL AQUEDUCTO. (The Aqueduct).— This has been, almost time immemorial, the water supply of the city. The system is the same all over Mexico, and a memento of the times when pipes had not been made, and people did better without them than they seem to do with them. Through its whole extent the arches are low, because the source also is, and as there is no pressure, the ancient and honorable guild of the water-carriers takes upon itself the hydraulic function. But each house of any pretensions to modern ideas has a force-pump in the area, by means of which to get a supply up stairs.

Throughout its whole extent, there seem to be no evidences of alterations or repairs, or that they have ever been needed. The ancient end of it is located in a most unprepossessing part of the city, and the stones of the basin are worn smooth and thin with the touch of human hands. The last arch seems to have ended in the street, and to have been left so,— 1677. But a hundred and two years afterward it was concluded to end the work in a fitting manner, and they added an ornamental piece,— 1779. Time was not then of much value in Mexico, and by the current opinion, is not yet. If *we* had built the same aqueduct, such a thing would never have occurred; it would not have stood long enough.

OLD CHOLULA.

CHAPTER VI.

THE VALLEY OF MEXICO.

THE list immediately following is intended to comprise points that may be reached by short and pleasant excursions by street car or railway, usually in one day from and back to the city.

The system of street cars in the Capital is very extensive and complete, and reaches all suburban points such as Tacuba, Chapultepec, Guadaloupe, etc. Other places, as Amecameca, at the foot of Popocatapetl, require a night's absence.

To strangers intending to make excursions to these places, and unable to speak the Spanish language, it is suggested that it would be advisable to be accompanied by an interpreter to show the places of interest that might be missed, and make bargains with hackmen, boatmen, etc.

As a passing remark, it may be observed that the street hack system of the city is under certain regulations that might be advantageously copied elsewhere. Each vehicle carries a small flag, either blue, red, or white. The color designates the quality of the hack, and its price per hour. When it is engaged the flag is taken down. You may tell at some distance, and without inquiry, quality, price, and whether it is already hired.

The mere mention of places gives the visitor very little idea of the interest attaching to some of these suburban visits. The glimpses of the true inwardness of Mexican life afforded by them are far more valuable and pleasant to think of afterward, than are the show places regularly kept in stock in most countries, and are by no means to be missed in a land so original and quaint as Mexico.

CHAPULTEPEC.—It is reached by street cars, but it is best for the first time to go by way of the *Paseo*; a drive which in the course of a few years will be one of the finest on the continent, filled with groups of colossal statuary, some of which are already in place, and lined with trees. The hill and woods of Chapultepec, quite indescribable in words, add to the interest which naturally attaches to it as a point of historical interest to all Americans. It was captured by assault September 27, 1847, and was an ugly hill to climb under fire, rocky and steep, and then as now, overgrown with thorns and brambles. It was originally a country residence, is now the national military school, and is under extensive alteration and repair, as destined to be the Executive mansion of the Mexican Presidents.

All around it was once a swamp, which the cypress trees took advantage of to grow to a phenomenal size. Some of them, double or treble, are about forty feet in circumference. Nearly all of the extensive forest of them are adorned with fantastic hangings of gray moss.

The monument to Juarez in the pantheon shows a genius for sculpture in the Mexicans. Another tasteful evidence of an appreciation of the fitness of things, is the beautiful monument at Chapultepec to the defenders of the place who fell in the assault mentioned. It is very simple, very unpretentious, and the plot of ground around it is exquisitely kept with banks of flowers and shorn grass.

Just beyond, and within sight through the trees, is Molino del Rey. The building is still there, but the place shows no marks of the fierce little skirmish that took place there immediately before the storming of Chapultepec.

Beyond Chapultepec, and reached by the same line of horse cars, is Tacubaya. This is a favorite place of suburban residence, and if visited during certain seasons of the year, will be found to be entirely given over to gambling and other orgies. At stated periods the authorities seem to think it best to turn the population loose.

A place opposite in character, and on the opposite side of the city, is the hill of Guadaloupe, and the village of Guadaloupe Hidalgo where the famous treaty was signed. It is the

home of *Nuestra Señora de Guadaloupe*, the
"Mother of Mexico." It is reached in half an
hour by horse cars, and people do not go
thither to gamble, but rather to pray. The
hill top is the scene of the Virgin's appearing
to the peasant. Everything here works mira-
cles, though I suppose it is necessary to believe it absolutely and beforehand, to have it
so. A corner of the fine church below, for
the largest edifice is below the hill, is given
up as a depository of canes and crutches,
votive offerings. There are several dozens of
tawdry little paintings, representing every
variety of accident by flood and field, each
with its misspelled inscription detailing the
miraculous cure worked by the direct and
instant interposition of "Our Lady of Guadaloupe."

It is, consequently, quite a health resort of
the very faithful, and not least curious among
the votive offerings is a tall stone tower on the
hill, made to imitate a ship's mast and sails.
There is also a curious garden or grotto, em-

bodying a local idea of beauty. The walls are entirely composed of broken crockery.

Interesting crockery of native manufacture is also sold at Guadaloupe.

TACUBA.—This is a village in the neighborhood, and a place of country residence for the more wealthy citizens of the capital. Near the hamlet of Popotla, on the way thither, stands the "tree of the Sorrowful Night" (El Arbol de la Noche Triste), beneath which Cortez sat during the whole of the night following his defeat by the Aztecs. The legend seems to be historic, and the remarkable tree is almost worth a visit, even if the legend were wanting. Near Tacuba is the famous church of our Lady of Remedies, much visited. There are also some interesting Aztec ruins.

Tacuba can also be reached by the trains of the Mexican National Railway, leaving city station both morning and afternoon.

CONVENT OF DESIERTO.—This is a ruined edifice lying among the mountain foot hills some miles west of the city. It is not reached by the cars, but is a good place to go for a picnic, the party hiring carriages as far as the hill, then going up the hill either on foot or by means of donkeys. The place is pleasant and the view from the hill especially attractive.

SAN ANGEL is a handsome and picturesque town popular as a country residence, and famous for flower and fruit gardens from which the city is largely supplied. There are pleasant walks in the neighborhood, and a fine view over the valley of Mexico. The factory village of Tizapan lies close by, and is interesting to visitors who are from the manufacturing communities of the United States. There is at San Angel a good restaurant near the plaza. The place is reached by horse cars leaving the Plaza de Armas every half hour.

CANAL DE LA VIGA.—This ancient water way is very well worth a voyage, as far as can be gone in half a day, at least. It passes through, or by, what were once the floating gardens of Aztec times, and are yet almost that. The means of the journey is either a scow or a canoe, preferably the former, upon the bottom of which you sit or lie, while it is "poled" up stream slowly by one or two Mexicans, who run up and down the slant of the prow. There are several villages on the way, and the jaunt usually ends at Mexicalcingo. Here is a half-ruined monastery and church, in front of which grow a group of enormous olive trees. The charm of this little trip is not quite explainable in words, but charm there is, and the Viga is extensively patronized by all classes, though foreigners sometimes come away without having heard of it. It is recommended to start as early as convenient in the morning, to buy fruit in the market place which is on your way, then for three cents a basket to put it in, wait there until a car passes, and go to the quay, hire a boat for the round trip, and eat fruit for dinner.

PEÑON DEL MARQUES.—This, from the city roofs, is a round mound rising from the valley some seven or eight miles away. There is an ancient convent there, in which there are hot

springs and a good bath. There is a fine view
of Lake Texcoco, and from the hill top also
a dim but interesting glimpse of the city.
There are various indirect ways of going
there. The best is to take a horse car for
San Lazaro in the Plaza de Armas and go to
the crossing of the line upon the canal ; there
hire a boat for the remainder of the journey.
Or you can remain on the car to San Lazaro,
and walk the remaining distance.

RAILWAY EXCURSIONS.

SAN JUAN TEOTIHUACAN.—There are here
some prehistoric Toltec (not Aztec) pyramids,
and other interesting remains. As there is no
restaurant at San Juan, it is best to take lunch
or fruit, unless you prefer to go to the neigh-
boring town of San Lucas for meals, where
there is a restaurant,—also a relic shop that
may repay a visit. The place is on the Vera
Cruz line and there are two trains every morning.

TULA.—This town is reputed among the

very oldest; an ancient seat of Indian rule. Here is also the oldest Christian church in the republic. There are ruins, presumed to be Toltec and prehistoric. The climate is perceptibly warmer than in the city. A detailed examination of the great Spanish drainage cut is obtainable here. There are two or three restaurants. Tula is a station on the Mexican Central Road, accessible by daily trains both ways.

AMECAMECA.—This is a quaint and picturesque place at the foot of Popocatapetl, and a favorite spot with tourists. There are many charming walks, and a hill called Sacro Monte, not far from the station, is covered with enormous cedars. There is a chapel at the summit and another upon the side of the hill. Popocatapetl and Ixtoccihuatl — the White Woman — overawe the place. There are restaurants and every convenience, and owing to time occupied in going, it is necessary also to spend the night there and return on the following day.

It is reached by going to San Lazaro, and there taking a train on the Interoceanic Railway, Morelos division. Trains leave in the morning.

TEXCOCO.—There are ancient ruins in this town also, some mounds, and the site and ruins of the palace of Nezahualcoytl.* A hill some two miles distant holds the remains of still another palace. A mile distant are the beautiful gardens of Molino de Flores. There is a fine old church. The place was in very ancient times a rival of Mexico, and is surrounded and covered by the remains of ancient magnificence.

It is reached by the Interoceanic Railway, Irolo division, taking street cars at the plaza for Peravillo. Trains leave in the morning.

The necessarily imperfect sketch of an interesting country closes here, leaving many things undescribed which it is hoped the reader may sometime discover for himself. Descriptions have been carried no further

* In these extraordinary names the author merely follows copy, and knows no more of their fluent pronunciation than the reader.

than was deemed necessary for the convenience of the intending traveller. There has been no attempt at tabular or statistical information. At best it is not uncommon for the travelling fraternity to differ from each other as to facts, to say nothing of impressions.

It is believed that as a field for the tourist and health-seeker Mexico has no equal, and there has been no attempt in these pages to conceal that impression. The facilities for a pleasant and economical journey thither are not overstated, and all ancient stories of danger, suspicion and semi-barbarism must soon be exploded by the experience of hundreds.

Not as a perfect specimen of the literary art, and not as a competitor with innumerable volumes published about Mexico almost weekly, but as a brief compendium of hints which it is hoped may be useful to the intending tourist, this little volume is left with the reader.

www.ingramcontent.com/pod-product-compliance
Lightning Source LLC
Chambersburg PA
CBHW032205010726
47493CB00008BA/2842